BENEATH A BLUE UMBRELLA

Beneath a Blue Umbrella

Rhymes by
Jack Prelutsky

Pictures by
Garth Williams

Greenwillow Books
New York

The artwork was prepared as full-color paintings
combined with a black pen line.
The typeface is Zapf International Medium.

Beneath a Blue Umbrella
Text copyright © 1990 by Jack Prelutsky
Illustrations copyright © 1990 by Garth Williams
All rights reserved.
Manufactured in China by South China Printing Company Ltd.
www.harperchildrens.com
First Edition 10 9 8 7 6 5

Library of Congress Cataloging-in-Publication Data

Prelutsky, Jack.   Beneath a blue umbrella.
"Greenwillow Books."
Summary: A collection of short humorous poems in which
a hungry hippo raids a melon stand, a butterfly tickles a
girl's nose, and children frolic in a Mardi Gras parade.
1. Children's poetry, American.   [1. Humorous poetry.
2. American poetry.]   I. Williams, Garth, ill.   II. Title.
PS3566.R36B4 1987   811'.54   86-19406
ISBN 0-688-06429-9

TO SARAH AND DOUGLAS
FROM UNCLE JACK

—J.P.

TO LETTY AND DILYS

—G.W.

CONTENTS

Beneath a blue umbrella
a melon seller sat,
selling yellow melons,
succulent and fat.

A huge and hungry hippo
made the melon seller mad
when he swallowed all the melons
that the melon seller had.

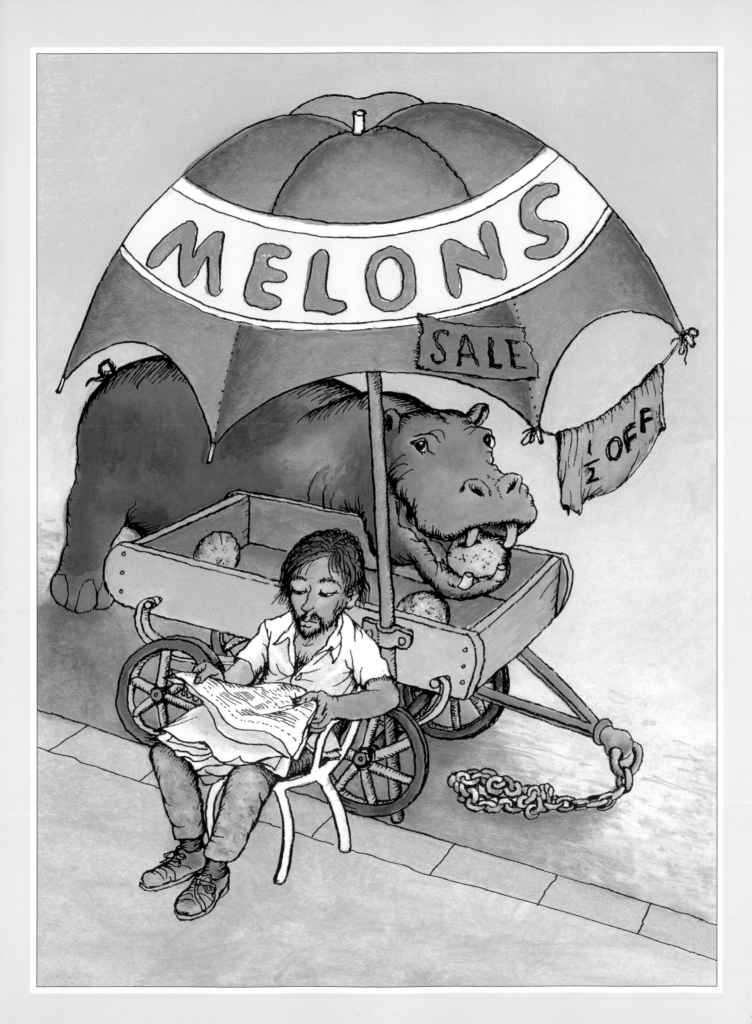

Rickety Pickety,
Percival Peake
rode a white bear
from Point Barrow to Eek.

He groomed his long beard
with an icicle comb,
then carried that bear
on his shoulders to Nome.

In a Mississippi valley,
on an old magnolia tree,
sat a mockingbird one morning,
singing loud and merrily.

Breezes carried off the music,
so that afternoon by three,
all the children danced together
in the hills of Tennessee.

Polly saw a butterfly
that fluttered in the air,
it seemed to be enchanted
as it fluttered here and there.

It fluttered by the hollyhocks,
it fluttered by a rose,
it fluttered up to Polly's face
and tickled Polly's nose.

Oh farmer, poor farmer, you're surely forlorn,
the crows have flown off with your Iowa corn,
they know your old scarecrow is nothing but straw,
they're feasting and boasting in chorus, "Caw! Caw!"

In downtown Philadelphia
upon a busy street,
three puppies found a pretzel
which looked very good to eat.

The first one sniffed it cautiously,
the second took a bite,
the third one snatched it in his jaws
and darted out of sight.

19

Jiggity jumpity jog,
a bobolink married a frog,
the little white mice
threw thimbles of rice,
jiggity jumpity jog.

John Poole left Sedalia
upon his blue mule,
the mule galloped fast
for the weather was cool.

They headed southwest
and the weather grew hot,
the mule became lazy
and slowed to a trot.

The day became hotter,
the mule would not go,
when John got to Joplin,
that mule was in tow.

I had a little secret
that I could not wait to tell,
I whispered it to Willa,
who repeated it to Nell.

Nell had to tell Belinda,
who told Laura and Lenore,
I think my little secret
is no secret anymore.

Four fat goats upon a boat
sailed south from Newport News,
and there the four ate clothes galore,
they swallowed socks and shoes.

They chewed on boots, on shirts and suits,
they shared a sweater vest,
a dozen coats went down those goats
before they reached Key West.

Robin spied a chubby worm
and thought he'd have a snack,
but when he tried to tug that worm,
it rudely tugged him back.

The worm was strong and sturdy,
and it pulled him off his feet,
so Robin thought he'd better find
a smaller worm to eat.

Idaho Rose, dressed in polka-dot clothes,
carries potatoes wherever she goes,
in one hand a sack, in the other a pail,
she calls out, "Potatoes! Potatoes for sale!

"Potatoes to bake and potatoes to boil,
to roast and to toast and to mash and to broil,
potatoes for salads, for fritters and fries.
Potatoes! Potatoes! Potatoes!" she cries.

31

Seven piglets, pink and gray,
who could not keep from squealing,
chased each other all the way
from Wichita to Wheeling.

Under fences, over rails,
they raced with one another,
then turned around and twitched their tails,
and hurried home to Mother.

Patter Pitter Caterpillar
high upon a limb,
looked at all the bumblebees
looking back at him.

Suddenly beside him
appeared a tiny bug,
and Patter Pitter Caterpillar
got a tiny hug.

Amanda found a flounder
near New London in the sound,
the roundest little flounder
that Amanda ever found.

Amanda snatched that flounder
and she tossed it on the ground,
but that roundest little flounder
bounded back into the sound.

Nicholas Narrow, tall and thin,
slumbered in a garden.
A sparrow landed on his chin
and chirped, "I beg your pardon!"

Captain Flea and Sailor Snail
went to sea in a plastic pail,
they were but a yard from shore,
when they lost their single oar.

Said Sailor Snail, "Oh, Captain Flea,
this water is too wet for me."
Said Captain Flea, "I feel the same,
I'm so sorry that we came."

A wave rushed in to wash the land,
it tossed them back upon the sand,
now they are content to stay
where the sea is far away.

Jennifer Juniper, where do you walk?
"I walk in the shade of a dandelion stalk."
Jennifer Juniper, what do you see?
"A grasshopper playing a fiddle for me."

Jennifer Juniper, what do you sing?
"I sing of the sound of a butterfly's wing."
Jennifer Juniper, where do you rest?
"On feathers and down in a
	hummingbird's nest."

Victor wore a velvet cape
and Kate a courtly crown,
Paul wore plumes and pillows
and Celeste a silver gown.

They laughed and sang and shouted,
what a jolly noise they made
as they frolicked in New Orleans
at the Mardi Gras parade.

Tippity Toppity, Upside-down Roy
was a remarkable upside-down boy,
he lived in an odd little upside-down house
with an upside-down cat and an upside-down
   mouse.

He never did anything proper side up,
he sipped lemonade from an upside-down
   cup,
his supper was upside-down butter and
   bread,
and he slept upside-down in an upside-down
   bed.

Red Bug, Yellow Bug, Little Blue
    Snake
floated on the Great Salt Lake,
they played and splashed without a care,
happy to be bathing there.

Big Green Bullfrog, mean and sly,
watched the three and blinked an eye.
"Croak!" was all they heard him say,
"Whoops!" they yelled, and swam away.

Johnny squeezed a concertina,
Fanny played a flute,
Benny tooted on a horn
and Winnie strummed a lute.

They marched around the Capitol
while playing songs so sweet,
that donkeys danced with elephants
on light and happy feet.

Anna Banana went out in the rain,
and walked on her hands from Montana to
   Maine,
she left at eleven, she got there at ten,
and then she walked back to Montana again.

One foggy autumn in Baltimore,
   Maryland,
Bonnie lost three silver beads by the bay,
they fell through a hole that she had in her
   pocket,
before she had noticed, the beads rolled away.

She searched for them all, but she could not
   find any,
it seemed they would never be seen anymore,
she found them that summer in South
   Carolina,
safe in a seashell upon the seashore.

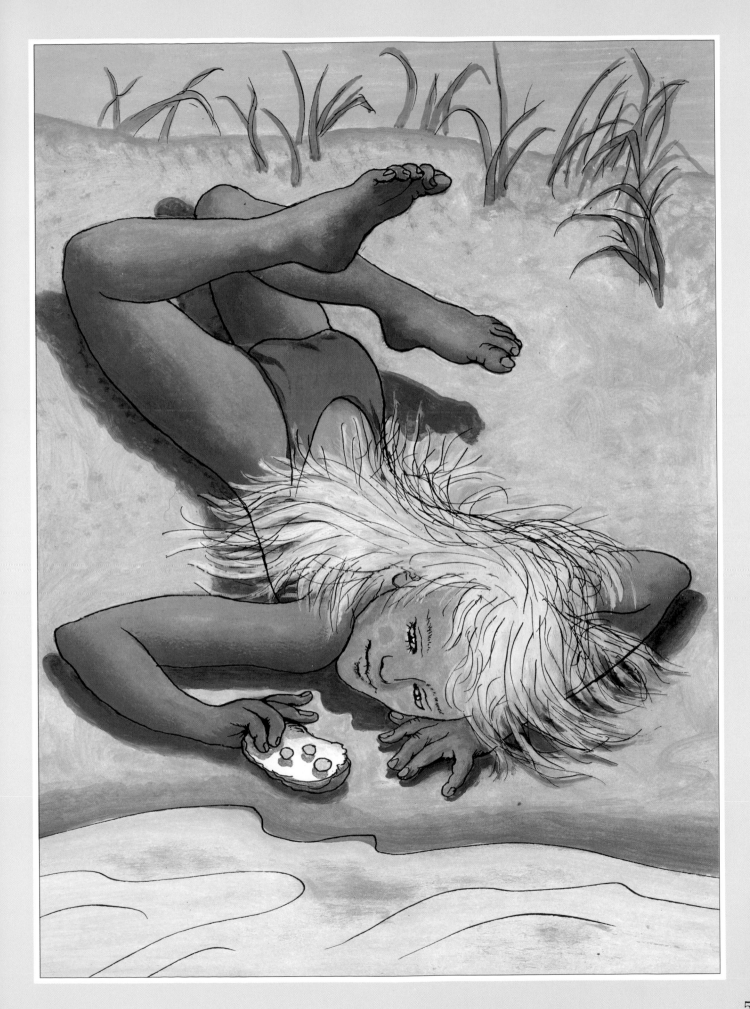

Tailor had a needle,
a thimble and a thread,
tailor had a square of cloth,
striped with white and red.

Tailor took his needle,
his thimble and his thread,
and sewed the gown and stocking cap
that keep him warm in bed.

Jason Johnson left New Jersey
just to dig for gold,
he tried in South Dakota
but he did not like the cold.

Nevada was much warmer,
but he found no golden ore,
so Jason Johnson headed home,
no richer than before.

I went to Wisconsin
to milk a round cow,
it made the cow mad
for I did not know how.

She kicked the pail over
and spilled every drop,
the next time I go there
I'm taking a mop.

Eleven yellow monkeys
in purple pantaloons
went to western Oregon
to play upon the dunes,
they whirled in dizzy circles
until they could not stand,
then grabbed each other by the tail
and tumbled in the sand.

Eleven yellow monkeys
wrestled for a while,
they tried a game of leapfrog
and landed in a pile,
by evening they grew weary,
and resting from their fun,
eleven yellow monkeys sat
and watched the setting sun.

JACK PRELUTSKY's poems are bellowed, repeated, and laughed over wherever there are school-age children. *The New Kid on the Block* received many awards and commendations and was an ALA Notable Book. And *Ride a Purple Pelican*, Mr. Prelutsky's previous collaboration with Garth Williams, was called a "modern-day alternative to Mother Goose" by *School Library Journal*. Among his other popular books are such favorites as *Tyrannosaurus Was a Beast*, *The Sheriff of Rottenshot*, *My Parents Think I'm Sleeping*, and his many beloved holiday Read-alone books.

GARTH WILLIAMS needs no introduction to book lovers. His classic illustrations for the *Little House* books, *Stuart Little*, *Charlotte's Web*, *Bedtime for Frances*, and *The Cricket in Times Square* are cherished by readers of all ages. His own picture book, *The Rabbit's Wedding*, has been in print for more than twenty-five years.